WE'RE DIFFERENT, WE'RE THE SAME

Featuring Jim Henson's
Sesame Street Muppets

by **Bobbi Jane Kates**

illustrated by **Joe Mathieu**

A Random House PICTUREBACK®

Random House 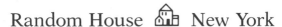 New York

Copyright © 1992 Children's Television Workshop. Jim Henson's Sesame Street Muppets copyright © 1992 Jim Henson Productions, Inc. All rights reserved. Sesame Street and the Sesame Street sign are trademarks and service marks of Children's Television Workshop. Published in the United States by Random House, Inc., New York, and simultaneously in Canada by Random House of Canada Limited, Toronto.

Library of Congress Cataloging-in-Publication Data
Kates, Bobbi Jane. We're different, we're the same / by Bobbi Jane Kates ; illustrated by Joe Mathieu. p.   cm. – (A Sesame Street pictureback) (A Random House pictureback) Summary: Illustrations and simple rhyming text show that while the body parts of various human and Muppet characters may look different, they have similar uses. ISBN 0-679-83227-0 (pbk.)
1. Human anatomy–Juvenile literature.   2. Individual differences–Juvenile literature.   [1. Body, Human.   2. Anatomy, Comparative.]   I. Mathieu, Joseph, ill.   II. Title.   III. Series   QM27.K37 1992   611–dc20   91-38545

Manufactured in the United States of America   10 9 8 7 6 5 4 3 2 1

We're different.

Our noses are different.

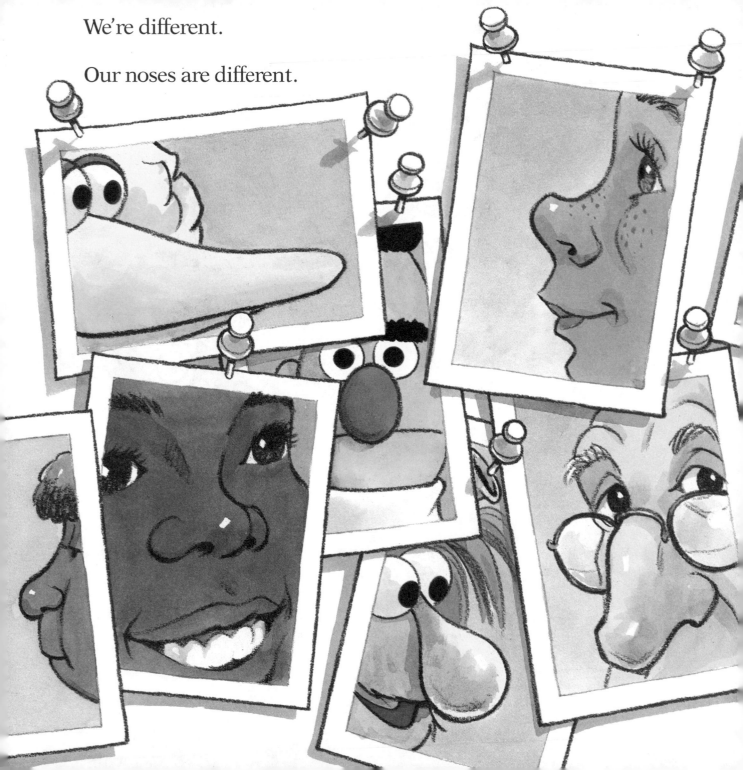

We're the same.

Our noses are the same.

They breathe and sniff
and sneeze and whiff.

FLOWERS
FOR SALE

Our hair is different.

Our hair is the same.

It grows on us in several places.
It warms our heads and frames our faces.

Our mouths are different.

Our mouths are the same.

Their lips form the words we say
and smile when it's a happy day.

Our skin is different.

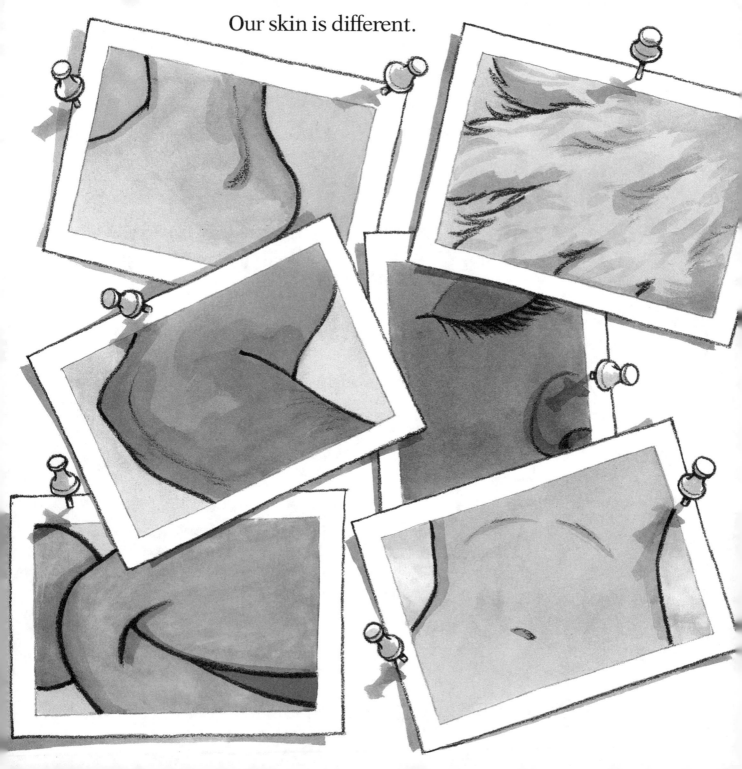

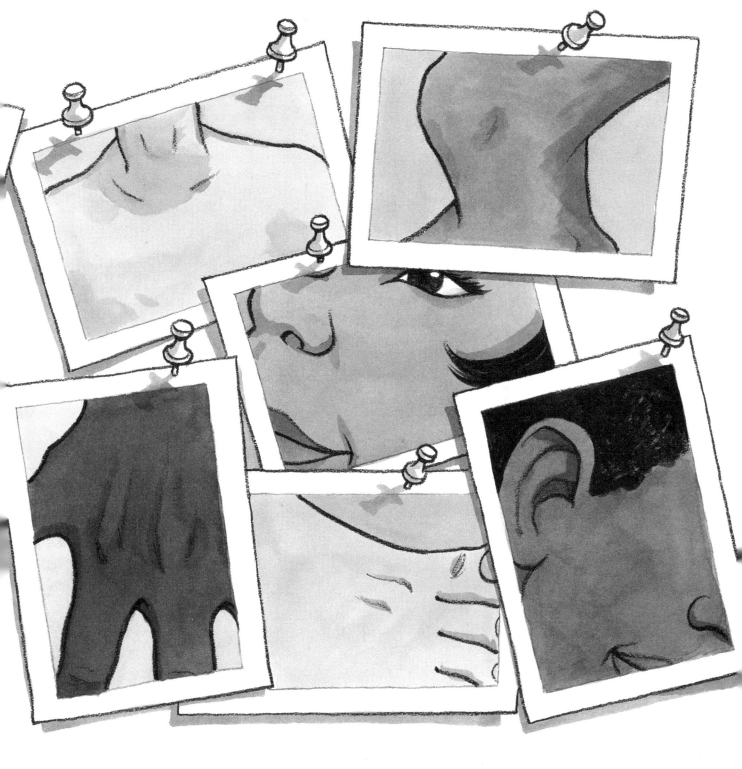

Our skin is the same.

It tells us something's cold or hot,
or wet or dry. It knows a lot.
Muscles and bones are wrapped inside it.
We all have blood and skin to hide it!
It keeps in warmth. It keeps out dirt.
It warns us so we don't get hurt.

Our eyes are different.

Our eyes are the same.

They see, they blink,
they weep, they wink.

Our bodies are different.

Our bodies are the same.

They stretch and bend and work and play.
They all need food and rest each day.
They dance and wriggle and ride a bike.
They might look different, but they're alike!

Our feelings are different.

Our feelings are the same.

Lonely, worried, scared, excited—
happy, loving, glad, delighted.

We're the same.
We're different.

That's what makes the world such fun.
Many kinds of people, not just one!
A rainbow would be boring
If it were only green or blue.
What makes a rainbow beautiful
Is that it has every hue.
So aren't you glad you look like *you*?

We're different.
We're the same.

We're wonderful!